The Black Swan and It's Adventures

By

John C Burt.

This is the story of "The Black Swan and it's Adventures'. The Black Swan is an Australian Native Bird .... And can be

found throughout the State of Western Australia. It is a rather beautiful bird , that is of course if one can get over it 's black color?

The Black Swan when it is born, is not much to look at ...but when it grows up , it becomes one of the most beautiful birds on all the earth ....

The interesting thing to note about the Black Swan is that it has red eyes and beak ... The two Colours which seem in opposition work on the Black Swan ...

The Black Swan is known to inhabit the waterways of Western Australia ... It can be an amazing sight to see the inland waterways dotted and punctuated by

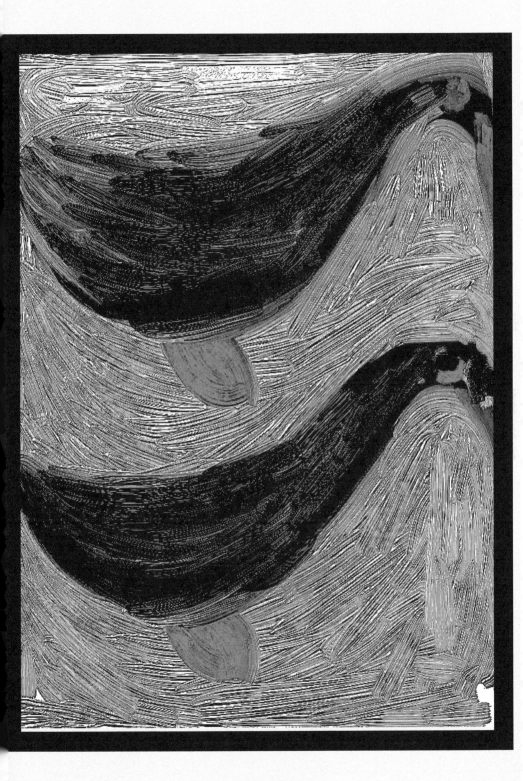

the Black Swans ..
It can be and is
a marvelous sight
to see .... The
Swans at rest and
play on the
waterways of the
land of Australia ..

The interesting thing to note is that you will usually encounter more than one Swan ... they come in family groups ....

The Black Swan is at peace and rest upon the waterways of inland Western Australia .... Yet it is a different story when they are on the land ....

When a Black Swan is on the land .... it can be and is very hard for them to get around ... They after all are birds of the waterways ... the waterways are

19

home to them ... to see them at peace on a waterway is definitely a sight to behold ... They glide effortlessly across the simmering water of the waterways ..

In some ways its like how people become familiar and at peace with their local environment and habitat .... So it is with the Black Swans of Western

Australia ...

Between you and me I think the Black Swan's of Australia look much better than their white cousins ?

I do hope you have begun to appreciate the Black Swans of Western Australia .... For the magnificent

**Bird they are ...
They are unique
to the country of
Australia ...**

Thanks ....

Lightning Source UK Ltd.
Milton Keynes UK
UKHW05n0813260618
324766UK00002B/17/P